GUARDIAN

www.guardoflegion.co.za

CHRISTO ROSSOUW

authorHOUSE®

AuthorHouse™
1663 Liberty Drive
Bloomington, IN 47403
www.authorhouse.com
Phone: 1-800-839-8640

Published by AuthorHouse   04/17/2013

ISBN: 978-1-4817-9110-6 (sc)
ISBN: 978-1-4817-9111-3 (e)

This book is printed on acid-free paper.

CHAPTER ONE

ORKNEY

＝ ＝ ＝ ＝

It is night time in a quiet, little mining town in the lower North Western province of South Africa called Orkney; a name that this little town inherited from a group of islands in the Atlantic Ocean. The sky was alight with stars as the Milky Way curled its tail across the horizon; not a cloud was in sight. In the distance a solitary jackal called out for some vocal company, a familiar sound to the inhabitants of this small town, that owes its existence solely to the large mining company that operates there and excavates its prized, golden bounty from deep within the earth's bowels. But the worldwide economic recession has crippled the mine and the once flourishing settlement was turning into a ghost town.

Most of the buildings in the civic centre was abandoned or labelled with to let signs.

A bar named "The Hole" was the only entertainment in town and it seemed to flourish under the current economic conditions. Out-of-work miners spend most of their days here and with poverty came negative elements like drugs and prostitution.

The Hole was also the place to be if you fancy too see some decent barroom brawls. Sometimes one unfortunate guy would just happen to be at the wrong place at the wrong time and get the living snot kicked out of him, by one or more hooligans that he has never seen before in his life.

Tonight was one such a night.

Outside the entrance of the bar, in the dirt, an unlucky, young man was kicked from side to side by a gang of five bikers that were passing through town. Spectators stood outside the door cheering, when sirens bellowed, followed by the flickering blue lights of a police van. The spectators and the aggressors quickly disappeared into the bar leaving the beaten young man lying in the dust.

The police van pulled up to the bar entrance and the passenger window opened, "Why are you laying in the dirt, boy?" The officer asked. The young man lying on the ground looked at the officer, still dazed. "It is time for you to go home now, ok!" The police officer remarked firmly, thinking that the young man was thrown out of the bar for being too drunk.

The young man slowly stood up from the ground. His shirt was torn and a nosebleed, packed with dust covered his face. The police officer looked at the battered young man, knowing well that he was assaulted. Without saying another word the passenger window of the police vehicle closed and it slowly drove down the street as if nothing happened. The trampled young man picked up his jacket from the ground and sat down on a step outside the bar. He took the sleeve of his shirt and attempted to clean the blood from his face as best he could.

"Are you ok, master?" A voice came from the shady corner of the porch. It was an old man, in worn clothes. He was covered in an old blanket and sitting against a wall with a bottle of alcohol in his hands. He appeared to be blind. The young man looked at him, "My name is Zack," he said.

"Are you ok, master?" The old man asked again.

"Yes, I am fine" Zack answered, "I am not your master, you can call me Zack"

"But you are my master!" The old man insisted. Zack shook his head in submission, thinking that the old man had one too many.

"Great evil is coming," the old man said in a blind gaze. "Only you can safe us!"

Zack looked at the old man and shook his head again, he felt sorry for him. The old man seemed to be senile. Zack stood up and placed his jacket over the old man. "Where do you live?" He asked. "Can I give you a ride home?"

"I will get by, master." The blind man answered. "You do not have to worry about me. You will have a lot to worry about." He added in a concerned tone.

"Ok, then." Zack said as he walked to his car that was parked not far from the bar. He climbed into the faded, red Volkswagen Beetle, and with a few turns of the key the old car started and he drove down the road on his way home.

"Evil is coming!" the old man on the porch said to himself. "I might be blind, but this I can see." He added, staring blindly into the night's sky. A light-blue glow started to pour from his eyes. "It is here." He said, an anxious expression on his face.

Zack was an only child and lived in a cottage on his parent's farm just outside town. As he arrived home, he decided not to go to sleep, because it was already past three o'clock and he figured that the little sleep would only make him more tired. He had an important exam that morning at six. A test that will decide, whether he will be employed by the mine or not. Work is scarce in South Africa, and his father had to pull a lot of strings to get him into this program that might ensure him a job. His father would be furious if he knew that Zack was drinking the night before this important test. The mine employed Zack's father, but after hours he worked on their farm to earn some extra money. His parents did not possess a lot of money and were unable to send him away to college after school. Zack didn't want to work on the mine, which caused a lot of friction between him and his father.

Zack laid down on a swing-chair in front of his cottage in the garden. He looked up at the stars in wonder. Never before has he seen them so bright and almost unwillingly dozes of.

CHAPTER TWO

THE ARRIVAL

He was awaked suddenly by the uproar of farm animals, the hauling of dogs and birds going wild in the trees. Looking towards the still dark sky, he saw a falling star or comet going over the farm. It shot down in the distance, not more than five miles away in the direction of Orkney.

Zack has always been fascinated by the unknown and unexplained; therefore he stares at the sky for a while longer, trying to recollect what he just saw. The falling object was about the size of a small car, pursued by a trail of greenish neon dust that spread like a swarm of bees, over the nearby town as the object made its descending flight. Zack felt the ground beneath him shake as the alien object made contact with earth. "Interesting." He said aloud, and made a note to himself to inspect this strange occurrence the next day. Feeling suddenly tired, he looked at his watch and saw that it was already half past four. He stumbled of to bed against his own advice, to get a few minutes of decent sleep.

The next morning he woke up late for class, the alarm on his cellphone did not go off. The effect of a head-hammering hangover follows this realization.

He jumped out of bed, and fell right over, he stumbling to his feet. He had trouble controlling his body and his co-ordination was completely off the mark. "What did I drink last night," he wondered. He rushed into the farmhouse kitchen, grabbed a bottle of water from the fridge and gulped it down fervently.

"You went out drinking again, didn't you Zack!" His mother says frustrated, entering the kitchen. "Your father is furious!"

"I don't have time for this mom." Zack interrupts, "I am already late. Let's talk later." He rushed out the door, jumping into his old car and rushes of. While he is driving, he kept a lookout for any sign of the comet that fell earlier that morning. He had a terrible hangover and gulped down big mouth full's of the cold water that he took from the fridge. The road was very quiet, he noticed. Even for this time of the morning. When he drove into the collage grounds at the mine, he noticed that only a few of his classmate's cars were there. "Maybe I am not so late," he says to himself turning into a vacant parking, next to a slab wall. As he made the turn, the rear wheel guard, smashes into a pole at the edge of the parking space and dents it all the way through. Zack jumps out cursing, "Damn it!" He curses, slamming the door shut and kicks the smashed wheel guard; unexpectedly the car slides a good meter away from him and into the car that was in the next parking space, the wheel guard was now totally demolished. Confused he ducks down and carefully looks around to see if anybody noticed what just happened. Around him were people watching him anxiously. Their skins were pale and their eyes bloodshot. They remained silent and kept staring Zack down. This continued for about thirty seconds. Zack, still in a ducked position, also stood motionless. His heart was pounding in his chest; he knew that something was wrong with these people. "I am sorry . . . ."

He started slowly standing up, "I did not mean . . . ."

Suddenly the weird spectators moved towards him in a stalking-like posture. Zack turned to run, but suddenly a white minivan came around the corner towards him. It swirled from side to side, intentionally running over the possessed people as it made its way towards Zack. It came to an abrupt stop in front of him. Zack stood motionlessly observing the action that was playing off in front of him. Then suddenly, without warning, the back doors opened and he was pulled inside as it spun-off at the same time.

CHAPTER THREE

DAY ONE

The next thing that Zack recalls is waking up, sitting in a chair in a place unlike he has ever seen before. It looked like a scene from a sci-fi movie. He gazed about for any sign of life, but saw none. With sudden realization, Zack grabs hold of his head as it feels like he still had a hangover. "What the hell am I doing here? How did I get here?" He thinks to himself. He looks around, and saw that there was a bizarre blue light present in the room that seems to come from the walls. It stirred around and lighted up the entire extent of the room. All of a sudden, Zack felt as if this mysterious life form was observing him. He stood still for a moment, and then walked across the room to the door, followed by the strange blue light. Suddenly the light started to twirl about him as he made his way towards the exit. An overwhelming feeling suddenly overtook him and he felt the light's urge to communicate with him.

He stopped; surveying the room in which he found him. An inexplicable, unfamiliar calmness came over him.

Against the wall, he noticed what appeared to be computerized screens, mounted into the steel like texture of the room. A large, circular window on the opposite side of the room came into his view; it was surrounded with unusual markings. The blue light drifted towards this window and Zack followed it. He expected to see space, but what he saw puzzled him. Looking through the window, he saw water. Light-blue water, like the kind found in a tropical lagoon. Within this water he saw old diesel submarines dating back to the Second World War, floating in the water next to the window. He could see the hulls of ships floating on the surface and airplane wreckages that lay scattered on the bottom.

Zack stared in amazement. "Where am I?" He wondered again. His thoughts were in disarray, but that did not distract him from the sounds he heard then. Someone was moving towards the door. He scurried about, looking for a hiding place and hid behind a column close to the wall. Emerging into the blue light was a being covered in a long brown cloak. The creature was about ten feet tall and strolled into the room with a long, walking stick. Looking about the room, searching, the tall being called out in a calm voice. "Zack, I know you are here . . . you need not fear me. We mean you no harm."

Zack remained still and observed the creature in silence. Suddenly though, the blue light found its way back to Zack and lit up the area around him, exposing his position to the tall creature. "There you are!" It said. "It is good to finally meet you," the creature remarked, looking in the direction of the column. Zack slowly made his way from behind the column, staring at the tall being in silence. He was startled when the creature removed its hood to expose its face; what Zack looked upon, was not at all what he expected.

The creature had a human like appearance, with a long, grey beard and big blue eyes that matched the colour of the strange light in the room. Zack kept himself calm, considering the predicament he found himself in. He started looking around, expecting more of the tall beings to appear.

"You are wondering if we are alone?" The creature said, "We are not. You do not have to be afraid here. This is my ship." He explained. "It crashed down onto your planet some years ago. My name is Sam." The being fell silent for a while, observing Zack's reaction. When Zack said nothing, he continued: "You have been brought here on my request. We have been watching you and the time has come for you to fulfil your destiny." The being smiled. "You, my friend, are the chosen one that will save this planet and the universe from a great evil that threatens its very existence."

Zack looked at him for a while, shocked by what he just heard. "Is this some kind of joke?" He replied aggravated, his expression a maze of unbelief. "Let me get this straight; first you tried to kill me, then you kidnapped me and now I'm the one!"

Three beings then entered the room. "Is everything ok here?" The largest of the three asked in a deep voice.

Sam

"All is well," Sam replied as calm as ever. "I would like you to meet the Guardian." He added, looking at Zack with great expectation. "The defence of the Earth is set. Zack, this is your team. At last you are assembled, alone you are powerful, but together will be infinite."

Meanwhile Zack stood in silence, listening to the tall being called Sam and wondering what to make of this entire affair. The three beings appeared to be human, but doubts clouded his judgement. If taken into consideration what has just been told to him, and that by a ten feet English speaking alien, he could not help but feel overwhelmed. The three humanlike beings watched Zack curiously. Among them was a big, tall man; at least seven feet in height, weighing well over four hundred pounds. Next to him stood an averaged sized man, wearing a black cowboy hat. The third was a girl that caught Zack's eye. She had long black hair, with striking green eyes and for some reason he found himself attracted to her immediately. She seemed very nice and smiled innocently all the while.

They were dressed up to their necks in some kind of shiny metal plaited armour. It conformed to their bodies, fitting perfectly, with the blue light from the room reflected of its surface. The big guy looked at Zack from head to toe, he smirked, then almost mockingly said: "This can't be him! Just look at the guy. We had to rescue him like a little girl this morning. He's pathetic. You must have made a mistake Sam, this guy's no Guardian."

"No Alex!" Sam interrupted sounding serious. "He is the one. Soon his power will be unmatched; he just needs to discover it. You must pardon Alex my young friend," Sam explained. "We have all anxiously been awaiting your arrival."

"Let me explain why I have brought you here. Two thousand years ago, my home planet—a star in a distant galaxy—was invaded by a great evil. My people were a peaceful civilization and we did not know war, but we knew that this evil had to be stopped. This evil force was an army of savages gathered from across the universe and ruled by a dark and powerful warlord that calls himself Malicious. His army travelled from planet to planet, destroying civilizations and recruiting all those who are evil to join his crusade. They created chaos throughout the Universe." Sam sighed, his grief evident. "A fierce battle took place on my planet, but my people were meagre in the art of war and we lost the fight for our planet. Legends spoke of a force capable of stopping this great evil. The Great Rulers of the Galaxy's created four immortal souls called the Guard of Legion. These four souls have existed for millions of years and restored balance and order to the once chaotic universe. That balance was now threatened once again."

He paused, looking at Zack intently before he continued. Zack listened, his interested piqued. "My kind was entrusted as the keepers of the Guardianship; the tools of power entrusted to these four immortal souls. It is written that the Guard of Legion is once again resurrected whenever evil threatens the universe. It was our responsibility to see to it that the Guard of Legion is equipped with the Guardianship. Without the Guardianship they would be powerless. Malicious knew that we were in position of the Guardianship, and seeks its power for his own. That can never occur, he had to be stopped!"

"I was one of the few survivors and was send by the elders of my planet to search for the bearers of the

Guardianship. I managed to escape from my planet before it was destroyed.

The elders on my planet made a crucial decision to destroy our world after all was lost, and efforts to stop the evil army have failed. They did this for the sake of all that is in the Universe, but they have died in vain. Although the explosion destroyed Melicious's ship, he was not, he was caught in stone and the ghostly spirits of his evil army now guide their master through space and time. Eventually they led him here, knowing that the Guard of Legion will arise from this planet that you call Earth. My ship was damaged by the explosive destruction of my planet, but I still had a mission to complete, the faith of the Universe now depended on me alone."

"After traveling through space for hundreds of years, I received an exceptional reading from your small planet and I realized that I finally found what I was looking for. After my ship got caught in your planets gravitational pull, it crashed down here, on an island between two landmasses, known to you as Bermuda and Florida. This was in the earth year 1403. My craft was badly damaged by the crash and could not be repaired on this, then primitive planet." Sam took a deep breath then, looking from the one to the other. The big one was evidently bored, having heard this tale to many times before. But Zack felt something stir within him.

"I did not foresee that my damaged ship would create an electromagnetic impulse, so strong that it created a rip in the space time warp." Sam continued. "This electromagnetic impulse pulled your ships and crafts that went through this rip in the space time warp to this island. The rip in the space time warp acted much like a one-way portal. Once a vessel has passed through, it could not return.

Because of all these vanishing ships and crafts, this stretch of the Western Atlantic became known to your people as the Bermuda triangle or the Hoo-Doo Sea. It was only recently that we managed to minimize the ripped effect, but this repair made travel through the *Space Time Warp* imposable for earth bound vessels, from both sides and sealed this island from the rest of the world. Over the years more than a hundred ships and crafts found their way here and I welcomed them. Some saw this island as a place to escape the war, while others saw it as a new beginning, away from poverty and slavery. Many however wanted to return to their lives and I gladly conveyed them back to their homes by means of smaller ships. There have been quite a few flights over the years. The sightings of these ships led to them being dubbed as UFO's by spectators. You are now on the once lost island of Atlantis. We all coexist here in peace. The humans that live here know about the immense evil that now threatens this world, and together we have created a great advanced army on Atlantis to do battle with this evil. By combining the technology of my race and your kind's knowledge of war, we have a chance at beating them. These three young warriors is the Guard of Legion. You my young friend, complete them. You are the Guardian and together as the Guard of Legion, you are capable of great things." Zack's mouth flew open. Sam smirked in response. "They have been here for a while now, training and learning to control their powers. The tall Guard's name is Alex, next to him is Todd and the girl is called Eva. She was born here on Atlantis. Alex is from New Zealand and Todd is from Texas, America. We almost gave up searching for you. Your energy reading took much longer than the other Guard's to surface, which made it quite difficult to find you. Your potential power only made its presence known when Malicious approached the Earth. Even then we were not sure if your force was positive, until after Melicious's arrival on earth this morning near your residence."

'That could have been what I saw this morning,' Zack thought to himself. 'The glowing green dust fallowing the comet, must have been the evil spirits?' In some strange way the alien's story actually made sense to him.

"Whether you want to believe it or not young Guardian, you are not a normal human being. Not anymore. You are exceptional in every way. You are the leader of the Guard of Legion; the most elite fighting force in the Universe and the faith of the human race depends on you."

Sam grew silent for a while; having what he said, penetrate the consciousness of the young Guardian before him. "The army of Malicious is rising as we speak. The beings that attacked you this morning are no longer human. The evil spirits of his warriors now possesses them. At this moment countless spirits dwell in the air around your hometown looking for evil hosts to bear their immortal souls and soon they will resurrect their master, Malicious. Only you can stop him Zack, no other can stand up to his might. Your power is growing young Guardian; I can sense it searching with in you. You must learn to use it, time is of the essence."

"He still looks like just another punk to me!" Alex said disgusted, looking at Zack.

"Yes!" Todd agreed as the two of them left the room. Eva didn't leave the room though; she stood next to Sam and listened carefully to every word he said. She seemed very interested in the newcomer. Another human, dressed in a grey uniform, entered the room and whispered something to Sam. "Very well," Sam answered him.

"Eva, please give Zack his Guardianship and introduce him to the island if you would? I have to speak with the Commander urgently." Turning to Zack, he said: "Good luck Zack." With that he exited, followed by the messenger.

"Don't mind Alex and Todd, Zack. They are not so bad once you get to know them." Eva said, smiling shyly. She walked towards a big glass case that was glowing with the presence of the blue light. She touched some of the inscriptions on the side of the case and the glass lid opened up. Inside was a silver metal ring and pendant inscribed with markings that glowed with the mysterious blue light.

She took the objects from the case before she addressed Zack. "This is your Guardianship." She said, holding the objects out to him. Zack looked at her with eyes wide, not saying a word. It seemed that he was still struggling to come to terms with all that has happened, and more over, everything that has been told to him.

"The pendant is your armour, just like the one I am wearing. The ring is your Guards' weapon. Come on, put it on!" She said enthusiastically.

Zack placed the ring on his finger; it fit perfectly. Taking the pendant next, he studied it querulously.

"How does it work?" He asked sceptically.

"You just have to think what you want it to do. It's like a limb really, once you wear it, it becomes like part of your body." She explained, "Come here, let me help you!"

The Guard of Legion

The Guardianship

She took the pendant from Zack's hand and leaned over to put it around his neck. Zack held his breath as Eva locked the pendant, touching him slightly. She looked into his eyes then, realizing that he was holding his breath all the while; she smiled, "you can breathe now."

Zack tried to exhale unnoticeably and blushed. "Try it," Eva said exited. Zack closed his eyes and concentrated. Nothing happened. "I don't know how," Zack said frustrated. When he opened his eyes, Eva swung at him with a whip, her guards' weapon. He fell back and covered his face with his arms. Suddenly metal scales started to spread over his entire body, from out the pendant around his neck, leaving the shinny blue crystal of the pendant mounted into the armour on his chest. His face was covered completely, yet he could breath perfectly normal and a blue crystal like lens covered his eyes. From the crystals on his armour a blue light radiated, the same blue light that filled the room and seemed to power the ship. This happened so fast that the armour absorbed the force from Eva's whip.

"Are you crazy?!" Zack shouted.

"Maybe just a little." Eva said in defence, although smiling. "It worked, didn't it? I knew it would do that. It protects you."

Zack admired the armour on his body, "it's so light and flexible," he said overwhelmed.

"And indestructible," Eva added. "What about the ring?" He asked exited. "It works just like your armour," she explained. "Sam says it's a unique sword, unlike any other. Nobody here has seen it yet. All the Guards have different weapons concealed in their rings and only a Guard can use this weapon."

"Don't even think about it," Zack said holding his hands out in defence. "I will figure this one out by myself, thank you." Eva laughed, "ok."

Zack studied the ring for some time and then he simply flicked his hand. A sword appeared in it. "See? No problem," he said to Eva.

The double-edged blade in his hand was constructed from a dark metal, with a blue crystal mounted into a silver metal handle. Zack swung it around and inspected the blade, then flicked his hand again and the sword disappeared once more.

"Impressed?" Eva asked.

"O, yes!" Zack answered.

It would seem that Zack was finally starting to believe in the bizarre destiny that the alien, called Sam, had foreseen for him.

"Do you want to see the island, now?" Eva asked.

"Yes sure, why not?" Zack said as they walked out of the room.

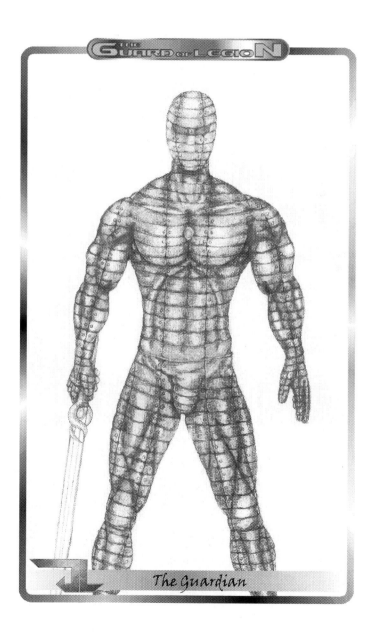

THE GUARD of LEGION

The Guardian

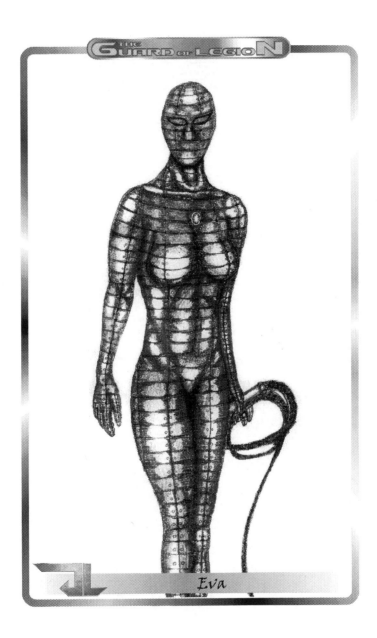

Eva

CHAPTER FOUR

DAY ONE

Zack saw many uniformed people as they walked through the ship on their way out. Some of them were operating computer like devices and monitoring screens. The whole ship seemed to be a defensive establishment of some kind. All the while, the mysterious blue light was ever present.

As Zack and Eva made their way out of the ship and into the sunlight, he saw the island of Atlantis for the first time.

"Do you know how many people have been searching for this island?" Zack asked. He turned around to stare at the giant spaceship that was situated on one side of the island; half of it was submerged under water. Although the ship was halfway submerged, it still stood at least ten stories high and spanned about half a mile in diameter. The island itself was very clean and neat, portraying a perfect co-existence between nature and humanity. It was civilized and seemed even more advanced than the cities and towns that he was familiar with. There were vehicles moving on paved streets and modern, constructed buildings. Rich plant live inhabited the city and surrounding area, with animals roaming freely. "They did it right!" He thought to himself.

Furthermore, old ships were stranded in the clear, blue water, close to the island. Children's' exited chatter could be heard, playing in and around them.

The island was just like a small city, only much more advanced. It seemed so peaceful, without any signs of poverty or pollution.

"How did they build all of this?" Zack asked.

"I don't really know. Most of it was here before I was born. There have been people living on this island for hundreds of years. The city of Atlantis was here even before Sam arrived. We have our own community and Sam is like a father to all of us.

His technology made it possible for everyone to survive here. He was the one whom gave us electricity; a system capable of turning salt water into fresh water and all the other luxuries that we enjoy. We even have TV," she smiled. "Just like you. Can you believe it? We watch the same programs, but we are not even living in the same dimension."

"O really?!" Zack said somewhat sarcastic.

"Sam is a strange name for an alien. He must be very old, with that grey beard and all."

"Well," Eva started "the story is that some of the first people that arrived on the island from an American navy ship, gave him the name. Apparently he looked just like the American icon, Uncle Sam, with his grey beard and blue eyes. They called him Sam since his name can not be said." Eva explained.

"Why? Is it against the law?" Zack asked interested.

"No!" Eva replied laughing, "It's just too damn hard to pronounce. Sam is a *Gigante* and on his planet they spoke a very complex language. He is five thousand years old. Time differs throughout the universe." She paused. Then continued when Zack said nothing. "I think his kind gets very old, because he claims that he's still fairly young. He sometimes tells us stories about his planet. He says that the elders on his planet were more than one hundred thousand years old. His people had no war or crime on their planet until Malicious arrived there. They also didn't have a sun in their solar system, but they did have a very powerful energetic live form on their planet that they co-existed with. This living energy gave them light and power, they called it Radiant."

"Wow! That is fascinating." Zack said amazed. Eva smiled. "True. It is even said that the person capable of wielding this energy would be one of the most powerful beings in the Universe."

"Why can't Sam use this Radiant against Malicious?" Zack asked, frowning.

"Sam has been trying to, but the energy is alive, it chooses its own bearer. The elders on his planet knew how to control its power." Eva paused, sighing as her heart ached for Sam. "It must be lonely and frustrating for Sam to be the only one left."

"This energy that we are talking about, it's the light on the ship right?" Zack asked curiously, noticing Eva's sudden grief as she thought of Sam's fate.

"Yes," Eva answered. "It came with Sam from his home planet."

"We have the same light in these suits," Zack observed; pointing at the glowing, blue crystal on his chest. "Does it somehow power this armour that we are wearing?"

"I don't know," Eva replied. "You should ask Sam about it."

As Zack and Eva walked through the streets of Atlantis, groups of people started to gather, greeting him politely.

"They know who you are Zack." Eva said. "According to Sam, you're our secret weapon in the war to come. He says that you're one of the most powerful beings in the Universe. The people feel safer now that you are here."

"What if I am not who you think I am?" Zack argued. "I don't want to let everyone down. They shouldn't rely on me." He said, looking at a group of children running around him."

"Zack, you wear the Guardianship. No one except the Guardian can do that, why don't you believe in yourself? Just take a look around you."

By now the streets where filled by gathering spectators.

"I'll tell you what, Zack!" Eva said out loud, "I will lead by example, a small challenge if you're not chicken. Watch this!"

Eva walked up to a minibus like vehicle that was parked on the side of the road. She took one hand under the bumper of the vehicle and without much effort, lifted the front part off the ground. Zack could not believe his eyes, that vehicle must have weight at least three tons.

"Your turn!" She said politely, placing the vehicle back on the ground. Zack declined, but Eva insisted along with the encouraging crowd.

"I can't do it!" Zack said frustrated.

"You will never know if you don't try." Eva moaned, pulling him by the arm towards the minibus. Zack slowly made his way towards the front of the vehicle and gripped the bumper with both hands.

"Go on Zack, you can do it!" Eva said, encouraging him.

He looked back at her and gathered all his strength; he gripped the bumper even tighter, closed his eyes and after a cry of tension, pulled upwards with all his might.

Zack couldn't even move the vehicle, but he was determent and kept on trying to lift the car, screaming. After a while, his efforts became quite amusing and some of the children started giggling hilariously, while their parents stared in disbelief.

"Concentrate Zack!" Eva said softly in his ear, "I believe in you." Zack concentrated as hard as he could; it felt as if every muscle in his body was being ripped apart as he pulled. Then, strangely, suddenly he began to feel very light, almost dizzy, as if gravity did not apply to him.

He slowly lifted the minibus of the ground using almost no strength at all. It felt as if thunderbolts were going through his veins. His strength knew no boundaries.

He laughed as he slowly placed the vehicle back on the ground. The crowd gave a sigh of relief. "It was only a joke," one screamed. "Thank God," another replied.

"Ok, show off, so you're strong. But can you do this?" Eva said to his back.

When Zack turned around to face Eva, he looked her straight in the eyes; this was odd since Eva was a good deal shorter than him.

Zack looked into her smiling eyes with amazement and then fallowed the vertical line of her body down to her toes. She was hovering in mid air.

"How do . . . ?" Zack asked amazed, but Eva just smiled.

Suddenly she shot into the air like a missile and swept over the nearby trees and buildings with the agility of a swallow. "Come on!" She yelled.

"How are you doing that?!" Zack shouted in her direction.

"Use your armour," Eva shouted, sweeping over his head, "think it to work!"

Zack closed his eyes and concentrated; when he opened them he was floating six feet of the ground. "Wow!" he said, mocking around uncomfortably in mid air. Suddenly Zack fell to the ground, "Oh no!" He shouted, closing his eyes again. Luckily he regained his concentration and stopped just before he hit the ground. "This is going to take some getting used to." He said to himself as he slowly rose to meet Eva. "These suites are really something," he commented, trying to keep up with Eva.

"Yes, its bullet proof, fire proof and water proof. It even protects you when you're not using it, and the best part is that you don't have to wear underwear with it." She said laughing.

Zack smiled shyly and pretended not to hear her.

"I'm starving." Eva remarked, "Let's go to my parent's house. They've invited you for dinner and I would really like you to meet them."

"Sounds good to me," Zack said. "Lead the way!"

The two Guards waved the crowd below farewell, and then set course to the residence of Eva's parents.

As Zack flew over the island, he could see just how big and complex the city of Atlantis really was. This mystical place was indeed a lost world, a paradise hidden from the rest of the world.

CHAPTER FIVE

THE POSSESSED

Zack and Eva landed in a road outside the city and walked up to what appeared to be a military base. There were soldiers by the hundreds training and exercising on the equipment in the yard.

They were definitely preparing for war. The soldiers were training in some kind of Hi-Tec armour that looked like gear from a Star Wars movie. Their entire bodies were covered from head to toe in a biomechanical suit and they were equipped with eccentric devices and weaponry.

"So this is what Sam meant by an advanced army?" Zack remarked. "What are we doing here?"

"My parents live here on this base; my father is the Commander of the armed forces."

"Oh!" Zack said, demoralized as he followed Eva to a big white house on the side of the parade grounds.

"Don't look so worried Zack." Eva smiled, opening the door.

When they entered the house, Eva's parents were busy in the kitchen preparing dinner.

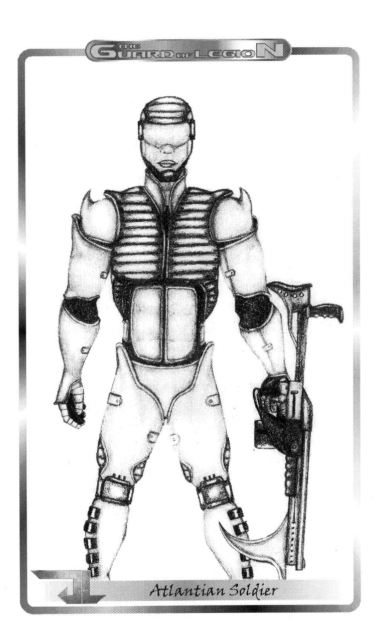

Atlantian Soldier

"Hello mom, hello daddy, this is Zack. Zack meet my parents."

"Hello Zack, it's nice to meet you." Her mother greeted politely.

Eva's father walked up to Zack and shook his hand. "It's nice to meet you at last son." He said in a deep voice, "Let's leave the ladies in the kitchen."

As they were leaving the kitchen, a little boy came running in through the door.

"Is this him?" he asked excited.

"Yes, now go away!" Eva replied.

The little boy ran up to Zack and gave him a good look over, "He doesn't look so tough." He said frowning and then ran off again.

Zack looked at Eva, "He's not mine!" She said defensively. "It's my little brother, Rob." She explained, "He's a very, very late child." She laughed, looking at her father.

Eva's father smiled in return. He was a rather tall man in his early fifties. He also wore a grey uniform with a lot of silver stars on the right shoulder. He looked like a man that demanded discipline. His short grey hair was neatly trimmed and his little moustache gave him that intimidating look about him. Zack followed him out onto the porch. The Commander placed a pipe in his mouth as he watched the soldiers training on the parade ground.

He then carefully lighted his pipe with a matchstick. "Sam hates these," The Commander said "He says it's bad for our health, we don't even make them here. This was my father's pipe." He explained. "He was the flight Commander of the first airplanes that landed here in 1945. Lieutenant Tyler, Charles Tyler, US Navy. You couldn't get this pipe away from him, believe me, Sam tried and my mother too. Too bad it's what killed him in the end."

"Dinner is ready!" Eva said, standing in the doorway. The Commander cleaned out his pipe in an ashtray on the table and they went inside to sit down with the ladies for dinner. They sat down in an old styled, dining room at a big dining table with place for six people. Zack couldn't help thinking how familiar it looked to the average dining room in the 'real world'.

"The food was delicious." Zack complimented, after wiping his mouth with a napkin.

"Thank you Zack." Eva's mother said, while instructing little Rob not to play with his food. Zack and Eva's eyes met constantly and it was easy to see the attraction between them.

"Zack!" The Commander said interrupting. "I hear you met Sam this morning."

"Yes sir." Zack answered.

"He can already fly and use some of his strength, daddy" Eva said proudly.

"Good. A fast learner, that's exactly what we need if what Sam tells me about you, is true." The Commander remarked.

Zack gazed at the Commander in a serious fashion; "Sorry sir if I am out of line, but don't you find some of this hard to belief, don't you find all this talk about Armageddon and ghosts a bit hard to swallow?"

"Zack," The Commander said with a grin on his face, "I grew up on a non existing island in the middle of nowhere, created by a five thousand year old alien; nothing is unbelievable to me. Although I can understand your doubts. Those damn possessed zombies almost got you this morning." He said as the grin on his face disappeared.

"They are disgusting creatures and extremely dangerous. The war has already begun and the battle is close at hand, we have to be ready for them."

"My dad drove the van when we picked you up this morning." Eva said, looking at her father.

"They are really something," The Commander continued, "There is no sign of humanity left in them. They will even eat one another if they have to. They are cruel demon creatures, fast as lightning and strong as hell." The Commander explained. "We captured two of them and locked them up in a holding cell, but it turns out they don't like to be placed together in confined spaces, so now we have one." The Commander paused. "I would like you to see her after dinner, just to get a glimpse of what you're up against."

"Her?" Zack said shaken. "Well, that's what it was." The Commander said. "Who knows what the hell it is now."

"Enough talk about those things for now," Eva's mother said. "There are children present at this table." She added, glancing angrily in the Commanders' direction.

"Yes of course," the Commander, says apologetically. "So, what do you think of our little island Zack?"

"It's truly unbelievable sir," Zack complimented. "Everything just seems so advanced, yet so environmentally sound. It's great! I wish things were like this back home."

"We hope there is some of that left," the Commander said concerned, rubbing his chin.

Suddenly Zack realized that his parents might be in the middle of what is to become the battleground for the war of the world. Luckily they are a few miles out of town, but were that far enough?

Later that evening, after dinner Zack, Eva and the Commander made their way to the holding cell, where the creature was held captive. Todd and Alex were already there when they arrived at the highly secure building. There were about ten armed soldiers guarding the entrance to the building, one called them to attention and they all saluted the Commander as he approached them.

"At ease!" The Commander greeted and all the men relaxed.

"Oh look, it's the punk!" Alex remarked when he saw Zack.

"Save it for the bad guys!" The Commander ordered as they entered the airtight building. They walked through a narrow hallway up to a big steel door. A guard opened it and they went in. There she was chained to a reinforced, steel structure in the middle of the room. She couldn't have been more then sixteen years old. The girl's skin was peeling from her body, leaving a slimy green colour underneath. Her hair was falling out and her legs was disfiguring into the shape that resembled a goat's legs. When she saw Zack she went crazy and screamed as she tried to break the chains that bound her to the structure. Something about Zack disturbed her senselessly. The demon girl suddenly paused and gave an evil laugh of frustration. She kept staring at Zack with her deep dark eyes, seeming very frightened and confused. Zack kept his distance, standing about five meters away, studying the creatures every move with a terrified Eva by his side. The sight was simply too horrific for her to watch. The girl then turned her gaze to Eva and in a deep dark voice she said, "He'll want you!"

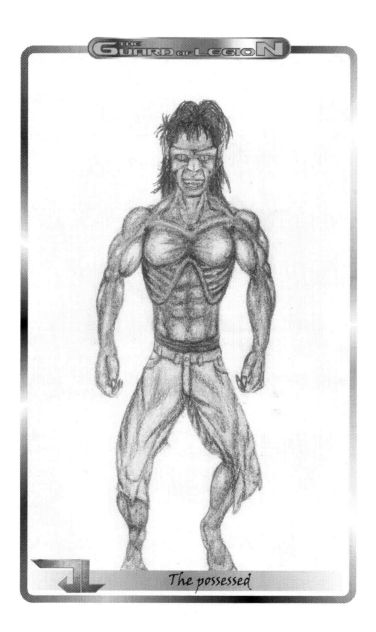

THE GUARD OF LEGION

The possessed

Eva grabbed Zack by his arm and held him tight. "Don't tell me the Guardian is afraid of a little girl." Alex remarked with Todd on his side as usual. "Yes, don't tell us you're afraid," Todd added. Alex and Todd pest and mocked the demon girl, but she ignored them and kept her eyes fixed firmly on Zack. The girl suddenly shifted her attention to Alex and started to laugh out loud again, "You're nothing," She said with an evil grin on her face. "You will die, just wait until the dark lord is revived, then all of you will die!"

"Shut your mouth!" Alex demanded, but the girl just went crazy again. "You'll die, you'll die!" She shouted, jumping around and laughing. "You will all die!"

The Commander tried to calm the big guard, but this outburst from the demon girl was more than he could bear. With a flick of his hand a big silver axe appeared and he chopped the possessed girls head straight off.

Blood sprayed from the demons headless body as her head rolled into the corner. The Commander looked at her twitching body and then at Alex. "You should do something about your temper son," He said aggravated. "It's going to get you into a lot of trouble someday."

Alex frowned in disrespect when he looked at the gory body on the ground; then turned around and left the room with Todd following close behind. Eva was traumatized by the incident and held Zack even tighter. The Commander turned to them, "You kids have to get use to this, you will see it again, no doubt about it. They are no longer human; they can't be saved any more." He looked at them, before continuing: "Don't show them any mercy, because they won't afford you any. They are possessed, now serving their master Malicious. You kill them by severing their heads from their bodies.

"Are you ok Eva?" He asked in a voice less stern. "I'm fine." She said still holding onto Zack.

"You two better get some rest," The Commander said. "We leave in the morning for the infest site."

The Commander bowed his head after Zack and Eva walked out. "How can I send these kids out into such a gruesome war, and my own daughter?" He said disheartened to himself.

It was already dark outside when Zack and Eva left the building. They walked side by side through the city to a boat docked in the harbour. There were children playing in the streets and couples walked on the beach in the moonlight. "This is my house." Eva said pointing at the big white boat, "What do you think?"

"I like it, it's different," Zack said.

"Well, let's go inside," she replied, "I'll make us some coffee."

"Now how can I say no to that? I really could do with a cup of the warm stuff." They climbed onto the boat and went inside to make some coffee.

The boat was a lot more spacious inside than it looked; it had a small kitchen with a bathroom and a little living area that he could see. "Where am I sleeping?" Zack asked curiously. "On the couch." Eva replied, bringing him his coffee. She looked at him and smiled. They walked up to the deck and sat on the side of the boat with their legs dangling in the water below. Zack held Eva as they looked up at the sky. It was a lovely night with clear skies and bright stars. The stars had taken on a whole new meaning to Zack in the last few hours.

"What else is out there?" He thought.

"I am scared Zack." Eva said.

"We all are." Zack replied.

"I have never felt this way about anybody." Eva said looking into the water. "It's so strange. I've known you for less than a day, but it feels like a lifetime. I just don't want to lose you now Zack, I want this to last forever." Eva said as tears formed in her eyes.

"You won't lose me." Zack said, holding her closer. "I'm here to stay."

"Promise?" Eva asked, staring into his eyes.

"I promise." Zack said softly and then he kissed her.

CHAPTER SIX

DAY TWO—MALICIOUS IS UNLEASHED

The next morning, the Guardians—accompanied by a small group of soldiers under the order of Commander Taylor—left the island of Atlantis for the small town of Orkney where the comet containing Malicious crashed down.

On the way to Orkney the Commander filled them in on their mission, "I belief in your abilities as Guards, but I don't want you to take any chances." He said, looking at his daughter. We don't know what they're capable of yet. You are to find the location of the comet, survey the area and estimate the enemy numbers only, is that understood?" They nod their heads in reply. "Study their movements and find their weaknesses, but keep a low profile. All we need is the co-ordinates to launch our attack." He explained. "What you are going to see will not be pretty, so be prepared and look after one another. You are all on the same team." He added looking in Alex's direction.

Alex gave Zack a swift glare, "uh," he commented displeased.

"What is your problem Alex?" Zack said standing up, "Do you have a problem with me or what?"

"Yeah !" Alex replied, walking up to Zack, "You are not supposed to be here, boy. You are not the Guardian and you're sure as hell not my leader!"

"I didn't ask to be here!" Zack shouted back in frustration, looking up at the huge Guard.

"Knock it off!" The Commander shouted. "You're stuck together, now get use to it!"

Zack and Alex stared each other down, then Alex turned about and walked away disgusted.

"This isn't good," Todd said shaking his head, "And they want us to save the world? Well good luck world, I'd say."

Later that morning, the ship set down on a cornfield outside the little town. The Guards, not wearing their amour to avoid suspicion, left the soldiers and the Commander behind and set out towards Orkney, hoping for the best, but expecting the worse. The road leading to town was deserted and the farm houses on the way where abandoned.

"Where do you live Zack?" Eva asked.

"My parent's farm is on the other side of town." He answered.

"Aren't you afraid for their lives?" Eva wanted to know.

"No, the farm is five miles out of town. Besides, my parents would have left town yesterday to visit my aunt in Johannesburg." Zack said assured. Almost an hour after leaving the ship, the Guard of Legion finally arrived in town.

It's been two days after the arrival of Malicious and his possessed; the town lay in chaos. It is likely that most of the residents got out in time, but the devastation caused by the possessed were still great. It was even more horrifying than any of them could imagine. Cars crashed into each other, buildings were set alight and bodies lay scattered in the wreckages. No sign of live was too insignificant to spare and even pets lay lifeless and bloody in the streets.

"Let's suit up!" Zack said, diverting his attention from the horrific sight and focusing on the task at hand. The four seemingly ordinary individuals simultaneously transformed into the Guard in an awesome display. "Let's move out!" Zack said taking the lead. As the Guards of Legion made their way through town, they saw death and destruction everywhere, but there were no possessed to be seen. The people seemed to have been taken off guard. The attack must have been very swift and sudden.

"These were innocent people!" Todd said angry, clenching his fists. "They did not deserve to die like this. We must stop them before it's too late!"

"Don't worry, Todd. We'll get them!" Eva replied, looking equally traumatized.

As the Guards walked through the streets, they approached a small park in the middle of town and inside they noticed the body of a man tied to a tree. The Guards were curious as to why this man was tortured in such a manner and went closer to investigate. The beaten body of the old man was tied up high into the tree with barbwire, his head hanging lifelessly from his body.

"Why would they do this to him?" Zack thought to himself. It would appear that the possessed wanted this man to suffer a painful death, but the question remains, why?

"It looks like they didn't like this guy!" Alex said, standing close by the body.

Suddenly the old man's bloody head lifted, startling the big Guard.

"Is that you master?" He spoke softly, "Have you come to save me?"

Zack immediately recognized the voice.

"It's you!" He said, "The old man from the bar. Let's take him off, quickly!"

"One of your friends?" Alex asked sarcastically, taking the man off the tree and laying him down on the ground. The man was in poor shape and he suffered from dehydration.

"I knew you would come to safe us master. There is hope now." The blind man said softly as tears of happiness formed in his glassy eyes.

"How did you know it was me?" Zack asked kneeling next to the old man, "You knew this was going to happen, didn't you?"

"I might be blind master, but I can see." The man answered, as his hands searched for Zack's face. He pulled Zack closer and whispered something into his ear. Zack slowly stood up, his face pale. "We need to get this man to the ship." He said, seeming very shaken.

"Eva," Zack said, "please take this man to your father's ship. You can stay there. We'll finish the mission."

"Can't we take him with us, I think it would be better if we stayed together," Eva argued.

"No, Eva!" Zack said in a firm voice, "I am the leader of this team and I asked you to take this man to the ship. Now what don't you understand about that?"

Eva gave Zack an unforgiving look, but took the old man in her arms and flew off without saying another word. Zack watched her take off, turned around and walked away. Todd and Alex was not impressed by Zack's behaviour, Todd ran up to Zack. "That wasn't cool man, why were you so nasty to Eva, what did the old man say?" He asked. Zack stopped and turned around.

"He said that all the people I love, would die today. Do you understand now?"

"What makes you think he's right?" Alex asked.

"He foresaw all of this. He tried to warn me, but I didn't listen and if he's right, there are thousands of possessed on their way to the crater site right now, if we don't stop them, they will resurrect Malicious. My parents may be in danger too, I have to go now!"

The harsh reality that his friends and family might well not have escaped this cruel fate, had struck Zack. Without saying another word, he shot into the sky and flew to his parent's farm as fast as he possibly could, followed by the other Guards. Finally he landed at the shambles that he used to call home. Tears ran from his eyes as he looked upon the lifeless, bloody bodies of his parents lying on the grass in front of him. The other Guards landed behind him and stood watching in great despair as Zack slowly walked towards their bodies. He fell to his knees, "Why God, why?" He shouted as his fingers impaled the grass, "Why!" he cried in frustration. "I have all this power and I could do nothing!"

It was clear that Zack was in a great deal of pain. Even Alex felt sadness and pity for Zack and rage towards the possessed whom were responsible for inflicting all this pain and grief to all those who came in their path. Suddenly, a snarling noise came from the wreckage where the house used to be. Zack immediately stood and walked straight to the spot where the snarling came from, with still tear filled his eyes. With every step he took, his tears of sorrow turned into tears of rage. As he walked through the doorway he saw a pair of dark eyes staring at him through a shadow in the corner. It was a possessed, eating from the corps of his pet dog. It looked at Zack, snarling and growling as he fearlessly walked towards it. Suddenly it threw down the corps and rushed towards Zack. With a flick of his hand, he severed both of the demon's legs from its body and it fell to the ground, screaming with its arms outstretched. With another swing of his sword he chopped of the possessed beings, grabbing hands. By now the possessed was no longer mobile and in excruciating pain. The other Guards looked on from a distance as Zack turned around and walked away, leaving the limbless creature screaming in agony. Zack walked out of the yard and into the field, and there he stood for a while just looking into the sky. It was almost dark now and a full moon was emerging into a bloody red sky. Zack tried to ignore the chaos in his own mind and focus on what was important. There was no time for him to mourn his loss, he knew that the decisions he made from that moment onwards, would affect the lives of every person in the known world. The burden that he carried was great. But he is the Guardian, the champion of mankind and he had to act like it. A great deal depended on him. He must keep the faith and be strong for the sake of the Guards of Legion and all that is live. Alex and Todd fallowed him into the field and stood beside him. "We'll get them Zack," Todd said aggravated, "I'll blow them back to whatever planet they came from!" With a sudden flick, his guardian weapons appeared and in his hands he held two bladed laser powered weapons marked with the blue Radiant light. "Just wait till they meet my two friends here, *In Charge* and his brother *Discharge*."

Alex was standing next to Todd, he didn't say anything, but one could see the anger in his eyes. The Guardians stood there in the field for a while longer looking at the night fall, then Zack spoke, "Let's go," he said, showing no emotion, "We have a job to do."

Suddenly and in true Guard of Legion style, the three heroes took off into the night sky and flew towards the distant lights of the small town over the hill. They swooped down over the town and through the streets, but there was not a possessed soul to be seen. "Where are they?" Zack shouted frustrated. "Have we missed them?"

They were just about to give up the search when Todd noticed some lights in the distance, just outside of town. As they approached these lights, they saw that they were indeed the light of fires set by the Possessed in the huge crater that was formed when the comet, containing Malicious, crashed down to Earth. From the air the Guardians could see groups of Possessed from every direction making their way towards the gathering site.

"Let's get them!" Alex said anxious, aiming at a group of about twelve possessed souls that were making their way to the crater. A burning anger filled Zack's hart, and a thirst for vengeance almost overpowered him.

"No," he said hesitantly. "We need to remain inconspicuous and finish our surveillance. There will be plenty of time for pay back."

The Guardians landed behind the crater wall and looked down upon the enemy. Inside the crater were thousands of possessed singing and dancing around the large fires. They were a bunch of savages. These creatures growled and snapped at each other, while pealing the rotting skin of their deformed bodies, revealing their true colours. In the middle of all the commotion, was the comet containing the dark warlord.

The possessed recovered it and placed it in the middle of the crater on a wooden structure that they have constructed from wreckages and trees. The comet containing Malicious was white and partially see-through, almost like a big block of ice. There was a possessed wearing a strange arrangement of skins and bones dancing around the comet and worshipping it. Suddenly the space rock cracked! All the possessed stopped their savage activities, and stared at the comet in complete silence. The possessed that was performing the ritual around the comet, stopped and placed his ear against the surface to listen for further movement. Suddenly a big hand busted through the rock and grabbed the possessed creature by its neck. The big hand simply clenched and the possessed creature's head popped off from its body with a gush of blood. This gruesome act made the possessed wild with excitement. With a powerful burst, the comet scattered into little pieces and a strong wind made its presence known in the crater. This wind twirled around in the middle, of the crater forming a miniature tornado so strong that it blew some of the possessed of their feet and forced the Guards to armour themselves completely to avoid sand blast to the face. When the wind stopped and the dust settled down, they saw him for the first time. He was unlike any being that they could ever have imagined. In the middle of the crater he stood, a nine-foot monster that would be more than able to haunt any man's dreams. He had large shielded, wings resting on his shoulders and a long powerful tail. The creature wore a bladed suit of armour and a metal mask that covered his entire face. The possessed celebrated and cheered when they saw their master. Malicious gave an evil laugh of delight as he admired his body. "Let's get him now while he's still weak!" Alex shouted with his axe in his hand as he flew like a bolt of lightning straight towards Malicious.

THE GUARD OF LEGION

The evil warlord called Malicious

"No Alex!" Todd shouted, but it was not enough persuasion to stop the big man from his coalition course with the monster. With all his might he slammed his big axe down on the head of Malicious, leaving the sound of metal meeting metal echoing through the crater. The seven-foot giant looked like a schoolboy compared to the likes of Malicious. Silence fell throughout the crater as Malicious stared Alex in the eyes. His head hadn't moved an inch from the impact. A chill spread through Alex's body as the consequences of his poor judgment and bad temper played off in his mind. Before the big Guard could think of making an escape, he was flayed to the ground, after suffering a massive blow from the monster's tail. With another powerful kick Malicious send him flying, but caught him again in mid air, with his powerful tail. He held the big Guard by his neck, and brought him up to face level. "A Guard?" He said, surprised. His tongue, an alien language. Alex was choking from the tight grip around his neck. It would seem that the giant's brute strength was even too great for the Guards armour to withstand. The possessed screamed in delight as Malicious swung Alex from side to side, increasing his grip with every move. Suddenly an unsuspecting Malicious was send plummeting threw the air and into the crater wall with a thundering blow from the side. An echoing cry of rage could be heard as the furious warlord emerged from the crater wall with a sudden explosion of soil. When Malicious turned around, he saw Zack standing in front of him. "Go Alex!" Zack ordered when a breathless Alex stood up from the ground, free at last from his nearly fatal encounter. The possessed encircled Zack and their master, expecting a brawl to take place. Infuriated static sprung from the ground as the two likely adversaries stared each other down.

"Come on Zack!" Eva shouted concerned from the Commander's ship that was hovering over the crater. The Commander decided to come and look for the three Guards after Eva returned by herself with the old man. The possessed were side tracked by the hovering ship and reacted by throwing rocks and objects at the vessel. Malicious looked up at Eva, "It can't be!" he said amazed, still speaking an alien language. The monster then fixed his attention back onto Zack again. The young Guardian slowly took off towards the ship above, not losing eye contact with the monster down in the crater.

"Till we meet again, Guardian." The large alien said, as the static from the ground around him died down. Zack just kept staring the creature in the eye, not saying a word, hiding the true fear boggling inside of him. Zack knew that he had to face this demon at some time, in the not too distant future, and this fuelled his fear even more. When he set foot on the ship, he looked down into the crater beneath him. There were thousands of possessed beings in and around the crater and countless more of their spirits were circling in the air. The spirits started to attack the ship in an attempt to snatch the body of a suitable host. Zack slammed the door shut just as the ship shifted into overdrive and disappeared into the distance, far out of the reach of the ever-searching spirits. The Commander made his way towards Zack and the other Guards, "Are you all ok?" He asked. After he confirmed that all was well, his tone changed. "You disobeyed a direct order and jeopardized the only chance we had against this menace. You were not to engage the enemy by any means, only to survey and gather Intel. What of that did you not understand?!" He aimed at Zack.

"It was me sir," Alex said, standing up from his seat, "I disobeyed your orders, Zack saved me. I am to blame."

"Well I am glad to see that your attitude has changed!" the Commander remarked. "It's worse out there than we suspected." He said concerned. The blind man was lying in a chair behind the Commander. "They will set out now," he said. "We have to stop them before they reach the big cities. The evil there will complete his army and then he will be unstoppable, even by the likes of the Guard of Legion.

"How did you know about . . . , who is this guy?" The Commander asked.

"He can see things Commander," Zack answered. "He is like a fortune teller, only he's been one hundred percent accurate so far." Zack informed the commander, before he turned to the man. "You are looking much better, old man."

"I will not be broken by evil, master," the old man argued.

"He just suffered from dehydration." One of the crew watching over him said.

"That's good. Now stop calling me master, just call me Zack"

"Very well, master, as you wish." The old man said.

"Zack shook his head in submission, his eyes constantly searching for Eva.

Eva sat heartbroken alone in the corner. Zack made his way towards her through the solders, with a guilty expression on his face.

He sat down beside her, "I'm sorry," he started.

"Hush!" She interrupted, placing her hand on his mouth, "Isak told me everything." She said, as she held him around his arm and rested her head on his shoulder.

"OH!" Zack said in a soft tone, stunned by Eva's reaction. "So his name is Isak?"

Meanwhile Malicious stood watching from the ground as the ship disappeared into the distance. Although he had wings, he hesitated to pursue. Could it be that the monster was too weak from his long incarceration, or did the power displayed by the young Guardian make him cautious? It would seem that for the first time this warlord has found an opponent to be truly vigilant of. Meanwhile the ship bared the characteristics of a beehive; all the soldiers were very curious and interested about what happened on the ground. Most of them were friends with Todd and Alex and interrogated them on the events that took place. Alex seemed very troubled and walked out of the compartment, ignoring the insistent questions from the crew. Zack saw this from the corner, where he was sitting with Eva, so he stood up and fallowed Alex into the passage. Alex was standing in front of a window looking down on the earth below. "What do you want?" he asked in a softer than usual tone.

"I just wanted to make sure you're alright," Zack said.

"I'm fine!" Alex shouted. A moment of silence passed. "But I would not have been," he said in yet a softer tone, "I could feel the life being squeezed from of my body, man. I never felt something like that before. Things like that makes you think about who you are and who you want to be. I believed that I was the one, I really did. All my life I was the biggest and the strongest. I had no equal, but I was no match for him, he would have K.O'd me right there. You saved my life man, you are the Guardian, and I know that now." He continued—smiling, "I owe you one, you saved my life."

"You owe me nothing," Zack replied, "but I would like your friendship."

"So, you still want to be my friend after the way I treated you?" Alex said surprised.

"Well, what can I say? I'm really desperate!" Zack joked. "So what do you say?"

Alex smiled while he looked out of the window again. "If you're that desperate," he said, "You've got it." He turned around and held his hand out to Zack.

"Ok then big guy," Zack said as they shook hands. Zack knew that it must have taken a lot of courage for someone as proud as Alex to admit to his faults like he did, and he respected him for that. The ship's crew stood in silence, amazed as the two once rivalled Guards, entered the room laughing and joking like old school pals.

"We would like to have whatever you guys are on!" The Commander commented as the ship prepared to set down on Atlantis. "Stay close Guards," he said. "We go to war in two hours."

For the first time, the Guards of Legion looked like a true team as they made their way off the ship together. It was clear that this experience has brought them closer together and the fact that Alex and Zack sorted out their differences, will count in their favour in the time yet to come.

They realized, that they had to be able to rely on each other, if they were to survive this ordeal. They didn't choose this destiny, but the fate of the world rested up on their shoulders now and they had to be strong.

"Would you guy's please excuse me?" Zack said as they made their way off the ship's ramp. "I have a few things I want to discuss with Sam before we depart."

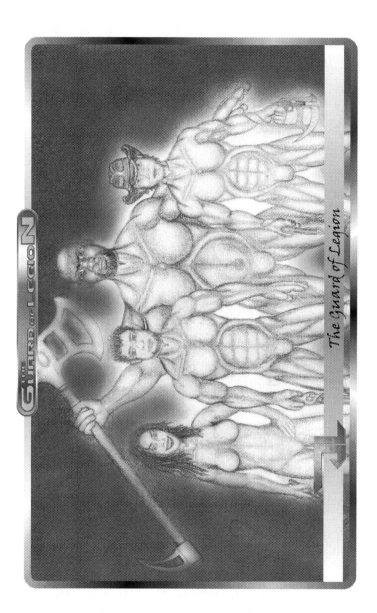

The Guard of Legion

"Yeah, sure man," Alex said, "We'll catch up with you on the ship."

Eva ran up to Zack and gave him a kiss. "Good luck," She said, "I love you too." She said softly. She then turned and ran to meet the others.

CHAPTER SEVEN

DAY TWO—THE FINAL BATTLE

Zack stood in ecstasy for a while, then he heard the Atlantian soldiers marching and getting ready for war. He made his way to the mother ship to see the alien called Sam. When Zack entered Sam's quarters, he was standing in front of a big window, looking down on all the brave soldiers, boarding the battle ships. From this window, high above the ground, one could see the whole island and everything that took place on it. Sam turned around and faced Zack. "I had hoped to see you before you leave, is there something that you want to know?" He asked.

"Yes. Actually there are a few things that I would like to know." Zack answered.

"Well, speak guardian." Sam said interested.

"Malicious and I had a little episode today." Zack started.

"You crossed paths with the warlord?" Sam interrupted, sounding very curious.

"Yes." Zack continued, "We had sort of a fight."

"Tell me more!" Sam demanded.

"When we were facing off, a strange feeling came over me, a feeling that frightened me. It felt like I knew him, like he was part of me. There were these sparks and static around us, and strong winds blew through the crater where he crashed down. It was supernatural. I could feel the energy running through my being and around me, it felt like I was going to explode. The whole ordeal was very bizarre. What does it mean?"

"Malicious is not part of you Zack," Sam said concerned. "You are a part of him."

"What do you mean?" Zack wanted to know.

"I will explain, but you have to listen very carefully to what I say. It's incredibly complicated." Sam looked at Zack for a moment, wondering where to begin. "Malicious is the Guardian." He said.

Zack interrupted. "You said . . . I don't understand, is there more than one?"

"No, there is only one Guardian and yes it is you." Sam explained, "Now listen to what I have to say!"

Zack looked extremely confused, but remained silent, carefully listening to every word that the tall, alien had to say.

"Two thousand years ago the Guard of Legion was called forth to protect the universe once again and so they did. This time, the warlord now known as Malicious, was the leader of the Guard. Only he was kind and well . . . . *normal ish*. He was the most powerful Guardian ever to emerge and a great and fearless leader that led the Guard of Legion into many battles, but such power as he possessed can easily corrupt the most decent mind and he got addicted to the might that he possessed. You see young Guardian," Sam tried to explain. "It is said that once the evil that threatened the universe has been neutralized, the Guard of Legion would have fulfilled its purpose and would so be relieved of its pledge and power. Malicious knew this and believed that the only way he could keep his powers, was by ensuring that evil existed. So he went on a rampage, destroying all those who were a threat to him and in the end he even executed his fellow Guards. His lust for power overcame him and he was changed forever. Malicious became evil in its purest form, a monster incapable of changing. He raised an army consisting of the most evil and dangerous creatures that the known galaxies could offer. He started to destroy one planet after another in his quest to be the sole ruler and most powerful being in the universe. The Guard of Legion was assembled many times from many different planets and civilizations, but every time it failed and was destroyed. The Guard were simply powerless against Malicious without the Guardian to lead them. A struggle started to commence within the dark warlord, with so much evil inside him there was simply no space for any good. You are not supposed to exist because he does. That is why we only came for you, the day of his arrival on earth. We had to be sure." Sam paused, contemplating, before he continued. "When he crashed here, the good inside him left his body and found its way to you. There was once a lot of good in him. There is good in all evil and evil in all that is good. You call this balance "yin-yang". You are both the Guardian, but the source of his power is pure evil and yours is good. You are equally matched in potential power, but Malicious is more than two thousand years old. He has a major advantage over you with hundreds of years of combat experience and he knows the full extent of his power. I want you to know what you are up against, young Guardian. However in history the power of good has somehow always managed to prevail over evil and we will trust in that. You are an extraordinary individual amongst your kind Zack; the power of the Guardianship seems to be growing within you. I have faith in you, now you must have faith in yourself. Is there anything else you would like to ask me?"

"Well," Zack answered, "I could understand the alien language that he was speaking and he seemed very interested in Eva."

"It's your suit." Sam explained. "It was worn by creatures, alien to you, that spoke a universal language, thus can you understand it. I can't think of a reason why he would be interested in Eva though." He said touching his brow.

"I have to go," Zack interrupted, "the ships are leaving." He turned to go.

"Trust in the Radiant, Zack." Sam said as the Guardian walked towards the door. "It will guide you and aid you." Zack turned around and nodded, unsure what the alien meant.

While the Atlantian soldiers were boarding the ships, the Army of Possessed was still growing as it marched from town to town destroying everything in its path and recruiting even more possessed. The South African defence force was powerless against them and the possessed souls easily overpowered a small unsuspecting army base along the way, while Malicious struck down the fighter planes that managed to leave the ground. At last a call for help was made to the United Nations after a disturbing *mayday* from the small, army base, not far from Orkney was heard. The message read that an assault was commencing from an unknown terrorist group and a united force was quickly assembled to help South Africa in its time of crisis. Meanwhile three thousand armed soldiers were taking off from Atlantis to South Africa, to fight the good fight for their home planet. When Zack boarded the last ship, the other Guars and the Commander were already waiting for him. "Glad you could join us," the Commander commented as Zack walked past him. Zack just nod and sat down with the other Guards. They were all very tense and anxious.

"Are you guys ready for this," Zack asked in an unsure tone.

"We're as ready as we'll ever be!" Said Todd.

"I am going to be honest with you guys," Zack said, "I'm scared out of my mind. You've seen those things we have to fight. This whole thing is like a bad song that I can't get out of my head, but we're here now. This is happening, whether we like it or not. We are the Guard of Legion, the protectors of the Universe and we'll be remembered forever. Sure it's a rotten job, but somebody has to do it. My family is gone, but I found something new to fight for." Eva looked at him. "Don't you want to be the ones that did it? Wouldn't you like to say I saved the world? I like to think that I got these powers for a reason that someone up there thought I could make a difference, and that they weren't just given to me by some random roll of the dice. We're going to save the world today guys, I know we can do this, I believe in you, I believe in us!"

"Yeah, Man!" Alex said grabbing the Guards and holding them together. The Commander was watching them from a distance and smiled in approval as the youngsters psyched each other up for the enormous task that lay ahead of them.

It was still night when the Atlantian ships arrived on the stretch of field were the battle was to take place. To the back of them one could see the millions of lights of the biggest city in South Africa, called Johannesburg, shimmering in the dark.

The Atlantian forces strategically chose this position and planes to make their last stand here, before the Possessed army reached the city.

Isak, the blind man, has foreseen this location as part of the route that the Army of Malicious will fallow and they will therefore pass this stretch of field to reach the city and complete their army. The Atlantian air surveillance has established that the army was indeed marching in this direction and taking the blind man's good track record, it seemed like the sensible decision to make. According to him the army will be millions strong after conquering the big city and then they will be truly unstoppable. This is the last stand and the only chance to stop this evil force. Isak was not allowed to participate in the war on account of his poor health and the fact that he was a valuable asset to the Atlantians. He was asked to remain on Atlantis, but he would hear nothing of it. "This was my battle long before it was yours!" he said. He then asked to be dropped off in a small town nearby when he saw that his pleading would not help. The Commander refused, but he insisted it be done as a last favour. The Commander gave in and he agreed to this, but on one condition; that an armed soldier to act as a bodyguard accompanied him. To this Isak agreed.

The ships landed and three thousand soldiers made their way on to the battlefield and started to position major weaponry and organize strategic attack points.

"Why are we fighting them from the ground sir?" Zack wanted to know as he walked beside the Commander, while he placed his men. "Wouldn't an air assault be more sufficient?"

"No Zack, we need to keep them together," The Commander explained. "An air assault will scatter them. When a possessed is slain, its spirit can still leave its body and find a new host, but if we keep them together, they will have nowhere to go. Their spirits always stick together."

"But wouldn't our soldiers be vulnerable, sir?" Zack asked.

"Don't worry, Zack." The Commander said in comfort, "These men have all undergone testing. They're good people and will be safe from the spirits. You should worry about the possessed ones."

"They are coming!" A soldier shouted after speaking on a communicational device, "They are approaching from the west!"

The Atlantian Soldiers took position in the surroundings and waited on the possessed army. The ground begun to shake as they approached. One could hear their growling and the rapid movement of their disfigured bodies as they came closer. Then they appeared over the hill opposite the Atlantian army, the moon was to the front of them and one could see their slimy skin, in the moonlight. There were more than thirty thousand of them against the near three thousand Atlantians.

Suddenly the possessed stopped and gazed straight ahead, they started to moan and growl as they pointed out at four figures standing in the dark, "It's the Guards of Legion, it's the Guard!" they said to each other. The four Guard stood side-by-side, their plated armour gleaming in the moonlight, motivated and ready to face this evil force. The Possessed opened up a path, as their master made his way to the front of the pack. The Guards looked upon the nine-foot monster, standing about two hundred meters away. They were all aware of what he was capable of, but they stood their ground nonetheless. They knew that it was their responsibility and duty as the Guard of Legion to stop this evil; none felt this more than Zack. He had a score to settle.

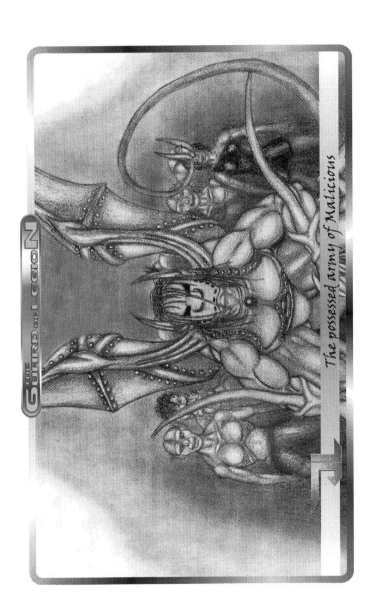

THE GUARD OF LEGION

The possessed army of Malicious
LEGION

Behind them was the Atlantian Army, concealed in the bushes, ready to attack.

They seemed terrified by the sight of Malicious and the sheer numbers of the enemy. The Commander saw the fear in the eyes of his soldiers and got up from behind the bushes and made his way to the front of his army. The Possessed watched him, anxious to attack.

"Atlantians!" The Commander started walking up and down. "Today we fight the most important battle ever fought in this planet's history." "Yes, we are scared, I know I am and you should be, we're outnumbered ten to one. We may not have numbers, but we have the Guard of Legion, we have each other to believe in, to fight with and for. We have humanity. What do they have? Just look at them! Today we fight for our families and the people we love. Today we fight for tomorrow!" He paused. "If they want this planet, they are going to have to go through us! By God we can do this! Are you all with me?!" He shouted.

"Haaaaa!" The soldiers shouted as they started to rise from their cover. Their hi-tech uniforms glimmered in the moonlight. Their suits and advanced weaponry were their only defence against a faster and more powerful opponent.

"Let's do this!" The Commander shouted, as the adrenalin pumped through his blood when soldiers rushed passed him to meet the possessed army.

The possessed responded and stormed straight ahead into the battlefield. Atlantian soldiers with fixed weapons let loose on the ferocious demons from all directions, it looked like two rivers running into each other as the army's clashed. The Guards fought paths through the sea of possessed with their superior strength and speed followed by the Atlantian soldiers. Most of the Atlantian Soldiers were armed with powerful bladed weapons, which they used to cripple the possessed and then sever their heads, using the blade. The war was gruesome and blood sprayed everywhere as the possessed heads rolled. The protective amour of the Atlantians gave them an advantage, but the possessed were exceptionally strong and fast and would succeed in taking down an Atlantian in numbers. They would target a soldier, take him down to the ground and shatter his armoured body with rocks or just about anything they can get their hands on. Zack fought with a vengeance and killed many possessed, but his battle was with Malicious and he was relentless in his quest to find him and bring an end to his rampage. As Eva fought her way through the possessed, she found herself standing face to face with Malicious himself.

"You!" He said looking at her as he tossed an Atlantian soldier through the air. A group of six soldiers fighting alongside Eva positioned them around the evil giant and started firing rapidly at the monster. The rapid fire from the Atlantians jigged off his body, causing no damage at all. The monster grew tired of the soldier's poor attempt and covered himself in his enormous wings forming a cocoon like object. The soldiers continued firing on Malicious, but in this form he seemed indestructible. With a sudden blast the wings opened and a strange energy wave send the attacking soldiers flying through the air. Eva stood shocked for a few seconds and then started lashing ferociously at the demon with her Guards whip, clearly causing some pain.

"Enough!" He shouted, grabbing the end of her whip, his tail leaped out towards her and snatched her around the waist and squeezed the air out of her. Eva struggled to get free, but she was no match for the monster's awesome strength and she eventually blacked out. Malicious then carefully took her in his arms and flew her away from the battle. Eva's father was fighting nearby and saw the monster taking off with his beloved daughter in his arms. "No!" He cried helplessly. Victory seemed so far out of reach as the weary Commander gazed across the battlefield. The seemingly endless army of possessed just would not fade and kept on coming back after every attack. "God help us!" He pleaded, giving a sigh of helplessness.

Then he noticed some lights coming over the hills from the right surrounding the possessed Army from the back. At first he thought them to be angels, but as they came closer he saw that they were indeed the headlights of motorcars coming from the distance; but they could just as well have been angels for they answered the Commander's plea.

Inside the cars were men crashing through the field, straight at the possessed, they ran over as many demons as they could possibly reach, hanging out of their vehicles with weapons and shot guns, firing wildly at the demon army that was retreating from the blinding lights. There must have been more than fifty cars, filled with allied fighters. For a split moment in time the Commander forgot about his crisis in the sudden, positive turn of events. Suddenly a red jeep stopped in front of him, running over a fleeing possessed in the process. As the Commander blocked the sharp light of the vehicle from his eyes, he suddenly remembered about his daughter.

"My daughter!" He cried, "He has my daughter!"

The lights dimmed and in the car were Isak, the blind man, and his bodyguard.

"I know, Commander," The blind man said gazing ahead. "Get in; we need to find the Guardian." The Commander jumped into the vehicle as it spun away.

"Where did all these people come from?" He asked.

"I wasn't always a bum, Commander." Isak explained, "What I saw years ago, is what you are seeing now. I tried to warn them, but they thought I was crazy. I wanted to forget what I saw, I didn't want to see anymore, but the visions just kept on getting stronger. I tried to kill myself and it left me blind. I lost everything I ever knew and loved. Everything has changed now, they didn't believe me then, but they believe now. It took some persuasion to get them here, they were unwilling to leave the bar on my say so, until they met my friend Steve over here," he said tapping the shoulder of the big Atlantian bodyguard driving the Jeep. I lived in the town nearby before everybody thought I was insane, but now they can see that I was not crazy, I was right all along." He said content.

"There he is!" The soldier said, pointing at Zack where he was fighting amongst the Atlantians. They stopped in front of the weary Guardian, leaving a cloud of dust behind them.

His armour was covered in the blood of his victims that lay scattered around him in their hundreds. As Zack slay the attacking possessed, the thought of his parent's lifeless bodies went through his mind. He remembered the disappointment he left his parents in and that fuelled his rage even more. He was now beside himself, a killing machine with one objective in mind. The total annihilation of the possessed army and all that implied.

"Zack!" The Commander shouted, jumping out of the Jeep. "He took Eva!"

Zack suddenly stopped. "What?" He said in a heated tone. One could see the fury in his eyes.

"Malicious took her!" The Commander said.

"Where did he take her? When?" Zack demanded to know.

"He took her to a big source of power in the west, Master!" Isak interrupted.

"What power source?"

"I am sorry Master, that is all I see." Isak answered disappointed.

Without showing any hesitation the Guardian took to the air with great speed, leaving a gush of wind behind. It would seem that his supremacy was increasing by the minute. He was finally starting to realize the true potential of his power. Meanwhile, Malicious landed in a big Power Plant not far from the battlefield. The workers from the Plant fled at the sight of Malicious when he casually made his way through the Plant, towards an open space. He carefully laid Eva down on the ground as she regained her consciousness. She was terrified when she opened her eyes and looked upon the daunting sight of the monstrous warlord standing over her. Eva crawled backwards in an attempt to evade Malicious. "Don't be afraid, Karnje," he said in a deep voice. "It is I, Malicious, come to me my love!"

"I am not Karnje!" Eva shouted, trying to escape the giants grasping arms. She crawled towards a building and got up to her feet, standing with her back to the wall.

"Don't lie!" Malicious shouted in a firmer voice, "Do you not love me anymore? I have endless regret for what I have done, it was not intended. I longed for your touch for so long. Now come to me!" He shouted.

Because of the Guards armour that covered her face and body, Malicious mistook Eve for his long lost love, Karnje. When Malicious was the Guardian, he fell in love with a female Guard named Karnje. They were deeply in love, and Malicious would have given his live for her. But his thirst for power corrupted his mind and he took his first step of changing into the monster that he is today. When he turned against the Guard of Legion, she tried to stop him and he took her live in an unintended moment of rage. He has since struggled to come to terms with what he did.

Meanwhile Zack was approaching from the east and one could barely see him at the speed he was flying. He stopped when he reached the big Power Plant. A strange feeling came over him. This feeling led him there. It was almost as if he could feel the presence of the monstrous Malicious nearby.

"A big power source," he thought to himself. "This must be it!"

The Guardian made his way to the ground in great hast. Just as Malicious bend over to grab Eva, Zack landed behind him.

"Don't touch her!" Zack said in a demanding voice, armed with the Guardian Sword in his hand. Malicious turned around and faced Zack. He started to laugh out loud and said. "You again. Do you have any idea how many Guards I have killed?"

Sparks of static came from the ground and the surrounding buildings once again, as they faced off, the electricity from the cables seemed to infuriate the static even more."

"I am not like the others!" Zack said, ready to attack. "You would be surprised to know how alike we are."

"Enough!" Malicious shouted aggravated. "You are nothing compared to me. You have pestered me for the last time, now you will die like the others!"

Zack took position and awaited the monster's attack with no fear.

"Why don't you stop your talking?" Zack said mockingly, "Or would you rather pick on the girls?"

With a furious scream Malicious stormed the Guardian, making his intentions clear. He wanted to destroy this character that dared to stand up to his might. Zack met the charging monster halfway and an explosion of static energy surrounded them as the two super powers clashed, creating a ballet of reflecting light in blue and green shades. It was a spectacular test of power, as the two supreme beings battled each other through the surrounding buildings and structures. They moved with incredible speed and it was almost imposable to follow some of their movements with the naked eye. Buildings and structures collapsed and buckled with the brute force of the battle. At first the battle's outcome appeared to be unpredictable and they seemed to be an equal match, but soon Malicious started to get the overhand. His strength and speed was simply superior to that of the Guardian. His armour itself acted as a weapon, the monster had two blades mounted to his fore arms, his fingertips were armed with serrated steel edges and his long tail acted as a lethal weapon. Soon the retreating Guardian was trapped between two solid concrete walls with nowhere to go. Malicious attacked the trapped Guardian with brutal blows to his body and with a final powerful drive he send the Guardian's sword swirling from his hand, leaving Zack defenceless to his attack.

Malicious took hold of the Guardian's neck with his powerful tail and started to slam him from side to side into the concrete walls that held him in confinement. The Guardian seemed powerless against this attack, and with a final swing he was send flying through the air and through the wall of a nearby building. The building started to collapse from the impact of the crash and soon the surrounding air was filed with a thick cloud of dust.

Malicious casually made his way to the collapsing building and gazed through the smouldering dust that filled the inside, like a predator stalking its prey.

There was no movement in the collapsed building; only the swinging of broken power cables hanging from the roof that caused sparks of lighting in the dark enclosure.

Suddenly the Guardian jumped from the wreckage and punches flew as he leaped towards the monster sending him stumbling backwards. The surprised warlord regained his balance and took a step backwards. A dark glare came from his eyes, and a greenish light started to emanate over his right arm.

Zack stared shocked at this phenomenon and did not know what to expect from the creature. With a sudden and unexpected blow from this arm, Malicious send the already battered and bruised, Guardian flying through the air. Zack plummeted to the ground. With great effort he emerged from the dust, busted, but ready for another round. No being could have survived this punch and Malicious seemed impressed, "You show great endurance young one," Malicious said walking towards the Guardian. "You are not like the others; there is something I like about you. I will give you a choice;" Malicious said "Join me and lead my army and I will make you more powerful than you could ever imagine. You will do this or you will die!"

"I will never join you!" Zack said in a vain voice, trying to keep his composure.

"Then you will die!" Malicious said, slashing the Guardian back to the ground with his long tail. Zack jumped to his feet using his last strength and launched a desperate attack on the monster, but he was too weak and his effort had no impression. Malicious grabbed him by the neck, leaving the Guardian's feet dangling in the air, with his deadly tail pointing at Zack's skull, ready to impale it. He laughed in pity as he pulled his tail back to give the final blow, "It's a shame to waist such a capacity for energy, but you are absolute and you must die."

Suddenly Malicious gave an unexpected cry of pain. When he turned around Eva was standing in front of him, "Let him go you monster!" she cried, slashing at him with her whip.

"You betray me again!" He shouted in rage, throwing the weakened Guardian to the ground. He started to walk towards her. "You have betrayed me again," he said. "Now you will join their fate."

Eva started to back away, but she stumbled and fell. Malicious strode toward her, towering over her, the tip of his tail pointing at her head. "No, you leave her alone; I'm the one you want!" Zack pleaded, trying to get up against a structure. Malicious looked back at Zack and gave a snort of spite as his deadly tail shot down and impaled Eva.

"No!" Zack cried as Eva gave a painful moan. Then there was silence.

He slowly stood from the ground as the armour around his face withdrew. "You have gone too far now." He said with his head facing downward. The earth started to shake and lightning crashed down on the plant causing multiple explosions and fires in the background. Malicious turned around, and suddenly felt a power unlike he has ever felt before. Fear started to grow within him. A strong wind started blowing through the buildings as Zack gave a demented laugh. "Your end is now!" Zack said in a deep voice, not of his own. He lifted his head to face Malicious. Zack had a grin on his face as the wind blew through his hair. His eyes came alight with the bright blue glow of Radiant. "You have killed everybody I love!" He shouted. "No more, it ends here!"

The lightning was crashing down with great fury now and it seemed to increase its rage as Zack's anger grew. A bright glowing object made its presence known, not far from Zack. It was the Guardian Sword. The sword glowed like a blue thunderbolt and increased its brightness with every step the Guardian took towards it. Malicious followed the Guardians every move with great awareness. When Zack took the Guardian sword in his hand a blinding light filled the sky. This flash of light could be seen from so far that even the soldiers on the battlefield paused and watched in amazement. When the light died down the thunder was still continuing. Zack took the sword with both hands, ready to strike and started to march in the monster, called Malicious's, direction. The monster felt intimidated by this fully powered Guardian that was walking straight towards him. He picked up a huge concrete slab from the ruins and threw it in Zack's direction. But the Guardian didn't even twitch and kept on walking after the concrete met his glowing sword and scattered into pieces.

"This can't be!" He moaned confused. "What are you. . . , where did you get all this power?"

"I am you're conscious catching up with you Malicious." Zack said, still moving towards him. "I am the Guardian"

"Impossible!" Malicious said outraged. "There can be only one and."

"Yes!" Zack interrupted. "There can be only one and your time is up."

Zack seemed very confident and the pure unadulterated power that he projected was mind-boggling. Malicious had never encountered such a powerful opponent and suddenly wanted to avoid confrontation. He opened his large wings and took off into the sky in an attempt to escape the young Guardian's fury. As he ascended into the sky, he suddenly found himself looking into the fist of the Guardian that send him plummeting back to Earth.

The newfound speed that Zack possessed was absolutely incredible, and it appeared as if the Radiant had rendered its energy to Zack, augmenting his power beyond belief. It would seem that the tables have turned now that the powerful alien life form has chosen Zack to be its bearer. What the young Guardian lacked in knowledge and experience he now made up for in brute strength and speed. When Malicious managed to pick himself of the ground, the Guardian already stood in front of him, anxious to continue the fight. Malicious immediately jumped up and launched a ferocious attack on the Guardian, but Zack stood his ground and blocked the attack without much effort. Malicious was becoming aggravated and his attacks became sloppier with every unsuccessful blow. Zack jumped out of the attack and landed on a structure behind Malicious, "Is that it?" Zack laughed mockingly. Malicious clenched his fists and gave a scream of frustration. "Come and fight me coward!" He demanded.

When Malicious turned to fallow Zack, he once again faced straight into the Guardians attack, which send him retreating. It became clear to him that the young Guardian's agility, now far exceeded his own. He covered himself in his large shielded wings in an attempt to escape the deadly attack. Zack attacked the cocoon like object with no successes. The monster's wings were indestructible, and the Guardian sword had no effect on it. It was this same ability that saved him from destruction when the planet of the Gigante, the alien called Sam's home planet, exploded with him on it. Malicious took this time to rethink his strategy of attack while the Guardian tried to penetrate the shell that Malicious hid behind. He knew that Zack physically outmatched him and that he had to make use of his knowledge and experience to combat the powerful Guardian. Suddenly the enormous wings sprang open and Zack was forced into a wall by an invisible wave of energy that the monster seemed to wield to his will. The Guardian was pushed through the collapsing wall by this force field that rammed everything in its path. Suddenly he was picked up from the rubble into the air and hurled through a building, sending the whole structure collapsing to the ground. Malicious screamed with satisfaction. Suddenly the wreckage moved and an explosion sent bricks and concrete flying through the air.

"Good one!" Zack remarked, brushing the dust from his amour. "What's next, mind control?"

Malicious held out his hands and blasted the Guardian with another energy wave. Zack intercepted it in an attempt to block it, but the force sent him stumbling back. He was pushed around for a few meters, before he took control of the energy and misdirected it, past him. Malicious was displeased by this and reacted by hurling a dozen energy waves towards the Guardian. Zack dashed towards Malicious, ducking the attacks as best he could. Just as Zack got within striking range from the monster, his body froze, leaving him suspended in the air and incapable of any movement. Zack tried as hard as he could to break through the force field, but it was no use. The force field that held him incarcerated, seemed impenetrable. Malicious casually walked around the struggling Guardian. "Stop struggling Guardian," he said, "it won't help. The force holding you is unbreakable, and it uses your strength against you. I must admit though, you were a superior opponent Guardian, but just like this planet you must meet your end." Suddenly Zack released all the tension he had applied in his struggle to free him from the force field and fell to the ground. Malicious stood shocked with amazement as Zack pulled back to deliver a lethal strike. He did not anticipate this move and crossed his arms in an attempt to block the attack. The impact of the blow was so great that it shattered both the blades on his arms, sending the monster falling to the ground.

He took a swing at Zack with his long tail, but Zack grabbed it, and now slammed him from side to side. Then he swung the nine-foot monster, through the air and sent him crashing into a network of cables and steel. Zack followed Malicious into the ruins left by the impact of the crash; broken power cables were lying everywhere and structures were collapsing around them.

When Zack entered the ruined construction, Malicious was searching aimlessly through the dust and debris. Zack suddenly stopped when the creature moved into the dim light. He had lost his mask in the impact and for the first time in thousands of years, his face was revealed. But the creature's appearance was not at all what Zack imagined. The monsters expression was undamaging and serene, almost like that of a child.

"This is not the face of a murderous monster?" Zack thought to himself.

When Malicious moved in his direction he stood his ground, ready to strike a blow. Malicious moved around on his four's, like an animal, snuffing as he searched through the rubble. His eyes were closed and it appeared as if he was uncomfortable without his mask. The blinded monster found his way towards Zack through the rubble and stopped in front of him.

Zack looked down on the creature as it sniffed in his direction. Suddenly the monster's eyes opened, striking fear into the heart of the unsuspecting Guardian. Never in his worst nightmares has he ever experienced such an evil glare. A growling mouth exposing a network of long crooked teeth, underlined these deep dark eyes that were staring at him. He made a dash towards Zack, swinging his tail viciously at the Guardian. Zack ducked the attack and moved in behind the creature. With a powerful strike he impaled his sword deep into the monster's back, in between his long wings. Malicious went wild with pain and fell to the ground, screaming and rolling around as he tried to remove the sword from his back, but it was helpless. The Guardian Sword seemed to burn him from the inside, as if it was taking revenge on its former master for his betrayal. Zack looked upon the disturbed monster as he rolled into a connection of broken power cables. Sparks flew as the swords handle made contact with the more than thirty thousand volts of electricity that ran through the cables. The Guardian Sword amplified this currant even more, making it lethal to even a monster as powerful as Malicious. He was screaming and shaking as the amplified electricity started to rip him apart. With a sudden explosion the monster's body was sent scattering through the air in smouldering bits. The explosion was so powerful that it flattened down everything within a hundred meters, leaving a craterlike whole in the middle of the wrecked power plant. There was no sign of live in the ruin that was once a large power plant, but then there was movement in the rubble on the edge of the large crater-like whole that was created by the explosion. A hand stretched out from underneath the concrete and reached for the sky.

It was the Guardian. He was still alive.

Zack cleared himself from the rubble and started to search for Eva's body. His weary eyes combed through the remains for anything that could resemble her. Just as he was about to give up, he saw a figure sitting in the far distant corner of the plant. He dashed towards it. It was Eva.

She looked up at him, "Is it over?" She asked in a weak voice.

"Yes," he answered. "Its over."

He sat down next to her and gave her a kiss. It was clear that he was happy to see her alive, "Are you ok?" He asked caringly. "I thought he killed you."

"He got me in the shoulder." Eva said holding her arm.

Zack carefully inspected the wound. It was a painful injury, but not at all severe. It would seem that the monster's intention was not to kill Eva. A warrior like Malicious is unlikely to make such a mistake and could easily have taken her live if he wanted to. Did he still carry regret for taking the life of his loved one? Could this monster have been capable of change, of feeling? Suddenly a bright green whirling light appeared in the hole where Malicious blew his last breath. It swirled around for a short while and then disappeared into the sky with a single flash, leaving behind the Guardian Sword on the ground, still glowing with energy. The Possessed on the battlefield all started to fall down dead on the ground as their spirits left their hi-jacked bodies, and joined their master on his way to hell. The Atlantians cheered along with their newfound allies as the enemy fell over on by one. They knew that the battle was over and that the war has been won.

Zack carefully took Eva in his arms and flew off with her to the battlefield where the other Guards were waiting on them, along with a worried father and Commander.

The sky was already a light blue, when Zack and Eva arrived on the battlefield. The Atlantians bid their newfound friends and allies a farewell as they boarded the ships to return to Atlantis.

Zack landed in front of the Commander's ship just as the rest of the fleet took off. The Commander was standing outside his ship and rushed towards his daughter when he saw her. He held her in his arms, "Are you ok?" He asked, "I was so worried about you, my child."

"I'm fine daddy," Eva complained, pushing her father away from her wound.

"Are you hurt?" Her father asked worried, looking at her injury.

"I'm ok, it's just a scratch," She said.

"Thank you for bringing her back to me, Zack." The Commander said with tears in his eyes.

Zack just nodded and gave a smile of content as Eva took his hand. The other Guards came running towards Zack. Alex picked the Guardian up on his shoulders and cheered while Todd bounced around like a little boy. Zack looked down at Eva as Alex ran with him into the ship where some of the soldiers were waiting for them. Todd picked Eva up and followed the other Guards to the ship. The Commander turned around smiling and faced the group of civilians that aided them in their battle. They were standing outside the ship. "Today is a great day and I must thank you all gentlemen. We are in your dept." He said. "Without you this night and this planet would've been lost. You have done mankind a great service and it has been an honour to fight alongside such noble men such as yourselves. Know that you will always have friends on Atlantis. I know that this must have been a unique experience for you," The Commanders tone became more serious. "But I must ask you to keep this encounter to yourselves. Some things are better left untold to the world. There will be questions asked about this night. People fear what they can't explain and they won't understand. This is human nature. Mankind lives an isolated live. Its content with its day-to-day existence, not knowing what tomorrow brings. Live, as you know it, will never be the same if you were to acknowledge every danger that threatens this planet on a constant basis. Chaos will overtake the world and the fear of tomorrow will drive humanity to insanity. We will concern ourselves with such matters. Let the world exist in peace, its better of not knowing when the end is coming. Do you understand this?" The Commander asked.

"We understand Commander," one man said, "I think your secret is safe with us."

"Yes!" Another shouted. "Who will belief a bunch of barflies anyway? I'm still so pissed; I don't even belief it myself."

"How are you going to get rid of the bodies?" someone asked. "We will take care of it my friend," the Commander said. "I thank you again."

The men then climbed into their vehicles and drove off into the dawn with blowing horns, but they left a man behind in the dust. It was Isak, the blind man.

"Take me with you Commander!" He pleaded. "I have nothing here. Let an old man life his last days in peace."

"We wouldn't have it any other way, Isak." The Commander said as he made his way towards the blind man. The Commander took the blind man by his arm and led him to the ship. "You are a very kind man, Commander." Isak said. "God bless you."

"Call me Charles," The Commander insisted. "You are going to love living on Atlantis."

The doors closed and the ship lifted off after all the men boarded it. "Set the co-ordinates for the Target, soldier." The Commander ordered. "Yes sir." The pilot answered as the ship hovered over the battlefield.

One could see the thousands of once possessed bodies lying on the ground beneath as the sun's first rays fell on the horrifying sight.

"Destroy it!" The command came.

Weaponry from the ship started to bombard the site where the battle took place leaving it covered in a thick blanket of dust.

"It is done," The Commander said. "Ok then people, let's go home." And with a blast from the thrusters, the ship disappeared into the sky, taking its passengers back to Atlantis

CHAPTER EIGHT

THE BATTLE IS WON—A NEW DAY

Only minutes later a fleet of U.N. helicopters lands next to the huge cloud of dust that still hung over the battlefield. Soldiers jumped from helicopters and took cover in the bushes in front of the dust cloud. The commanding officer made his way to the front, "Is this it?" He asks, studying the dust cloud.

"Yes sir, this is the co-ordinates." A soldier answered, checking a map as he walks into the dust cloud. Suddenly the commanding officer grabs him by his shirt and pulls him back.

The frightened soldier looked at his superior with uncertainty. The officer did not say a word. He just stared into the dust cloud in front of him. When the soldier looked through the dust, he saw that they were standing on the edge of a deep canyon like hole. This was created by the blasts form the Atlantian ship.

"Whatever did this is not here anymore." The commanding officer said, "This is like a story from the Bermuda triangle."

Meanwhile on Atlantis the victorious soldiers were returning from the battle. The whole of Atlantis was waiting on them as they set down on the landing pads. The Atlantians cheered the soldiers on when they made their way of the ships, but one could not help to see the sadness in their eyes when the dead and wounded were carried off. There was great excitement among the people when the commanding ship arrived and the children stormed the Guards as they made their way of the ramp. Sam was waiting at the end to meet them.

"Well done Guard of Legion," he said as they met him. "You have fulfilled you're destiny, and made me proud to be the Keeper."

Alex walked up to Sam. "There is something wrong with my Guardianship, its losing power." He said

"This does not surprise me." Sam said, "There is no need for it to work because the evil that threatened all has been eliminated, therefore you are relieved from your obligation as the Guard of Legion until evil threatens the balance of the universe once more."

"Oh?" Alex said confused, "Just like that?"

"Yes, Alex." Sam said, "Just like that."

"I think it would be wise if I took the Guardianship and returned it to its holding place where it will be safe until the time comes once again when it is needed."

The Guard of Legion relived their armour and handed their Guardianship over to Sam with a strange sadness, overpowered by relief.

"You can rest now young Guards," Sam said. "You have deserved it."

"Rest!" Todd shouted outraged, "not me. I'm a party animal!"

"I'm with you little man," Alex said, "Are you going to join us Zack?"

"Sorry guys, I will catch up later," Zack said.

"It's your loss man!" Todd shouted as he and Alex ran into the crowd. They were obviously relieved to be back and wanted to celebrate the victory with their friends. Sam looked at the blind man standing next to the Commander, "Isak?!" He said surprised. "You are back"

"Hallo Sam." Isak said smiling.

"It looks like you two have a lot to talk about." The Commander said excusing himself from the conversation. He turned his attention to Zack and Eva.

"We have to get you to a doctor so that he can take a look at that wound, Eva." He said caringly.

"I'm fine, Daddy." Eva said holding on to Zack.

"Your father is right Eva. Go with him, I will see you later." Zack said kissing her on her forehead.

"Do you promise?" She asked.

"I promise." He answered, "I am not going anywhere."

Zack watched Eva and her father as they walked away; he then made his way through the people with a content smile on his face. He walked through the cheering crowd and left them behind with a troubled mind. As the Guardian, he didn't have time to reflect on his personal needs and now he was left with a lot of emotional issues. He was troubled by the death of his friends and parents, by Eva's encounter and the bloodshed that he witnessed and so easily applied. Zack walked around for hours until it was dark. As he walked through Atlantis, he saw that the people were happy and merry and there were parties everywhere to celebrate the victory. Zack walked up to Eva's parent's house. They were having a barbeque with some friends in the front yard. They cheered and greeted the young Guardian when they saw him. Eva's mother walked up to Zack, "She is in her room." She said softly, "She is sleeping, but she wouldn't mind to see you."

"Thank you, ma'am." Zack said.

"No," She said giving him a hug, "thank you."

When Zack entered the room, he saw his love lying on the bed. She seemed so peaceful and careless where she lay and he did not want to wake her. She was without a doubt, the most beautiful thing that he has ever seen. He sat down next to her and kissed her softly, "I promised." He said.

The guardian felt more content and satisfied with himself as he walked out of the house.

"Join us Zack!" The Commander said.

"I will see you later sir. There is something that I have to do first." Zack replied.

Zack saw fireworks in the sky as he left the yard on his way to the beach. He walked up to a secluded stretch of sand and looked around for people. Then gazed up at the sky and smiled. He knew that his parents were up there somewhere and that they were proud of him for once. He grinned as a blue glow came to his eyes once again and he suddenly leaped into the air and flew over the water. The Guardian laughed with satisfaction as he spun around in the air and dived through the water. Sam was standing in his ship, looking down on Zack from the big window in his quarters.

"At last the right soul has the power." He said content.

"I told you so." Isak said laughing on a couch behind the alien.

The End

EPILOGUE

Zack is the Guardian and one of the most powerful beings in existence. This once ordinary young man, now champions humanity and leads the most elite fighting force in the Universe. Together the Guard of Legion have overcome the odds and saved the Earth as well as the Universe from certain chaos and destruction.

This is only the beginning though of a new legend. The Guard of Legion were called forth many times more and lived on to have countless more adventures, but that's another story, for another time.